TIMBERWOLF Revenge

Sigmund Brouwer
illustrations by Dean Griffiths

ORCA BOOK PUBLISHERS

Library and Archives Canada Cataloguing in Publication

Brouwer, Sigmund, 1959-

Timberwolf revenge / Sigmund Brouwer; illustrations by Dean Griffiths.

(Orca echoes)

(Howling Timberwolves series)

ISBN 1-55143-544-6

I. Title. II. Series. III. Series: Brouwer, Sigmund, 1959- . Howling Timberwolves series.

PS8553.R68467T547 2006   jC813'.54   C2006-903016-2

Library of Congress Control Number: 2006927108

Summary: Hockey action and humor that will appeal to young readers.

Orca Book Publishers gratefully acknowledges the support for its publishing programs provided by the
following agencies: the Government of Canada through the Book Publishing Industry Development
Program and the Canada Council for the Arts, and the Province of British Columbia through the
BC Arts Council and the Book Publishing Tax Credit.

Design and typesetting by Doug McCaffry

Cover and interior illustrations by Dean Griffiths

Orca Book Publishers
PO Box 5626 Stn. B
Victoria, BC Canada
V8R 6S4

Orca Book Publishers
PO Box 468
Custer, WA USA
98240-0468

Printed and bound in Canada.

Printed on recycled paper, 60% PCW.

09 08 07 06 • 4 3 2 1

To Walter Tarnowsky and his beloved Leafs—D.G.

CHAPTER ONE

Johnny Maverick kicked open the door of the dressing room. The door nearly hit Coach Smith.

"Hey," Coach Smith said. "Watch out."

"I'm sorry," Johnny said. He was a center on the Howling Timberwolves hockey team. "But I just lost two loonies."

Everybody on the team looked up from putting on their equipment. Some were already tying skates. They were getting ready for a big game.

"How could you lose two loonies?" Coach Smith said. "All you did was go into the bathroom on the other side of that door."

"I was pulling my coat off," Johnny answered. He shook his coat. It jingled. "See? I had a whole bunch of change in my pocket. Two loonies fell out."

"So pick them up," Coach Smith said.

"They fell into the toilet," Johnny said.

Everyone on the team laughed. The Timberwolves all lived in a small town called Howling. They were in Calgary for a big hockey tournament.

"Are the two loonies still in the toilet?" Coach Smith asked.

"Yes," Johnny said. "Right on the bottom."

Everyone laughed again.

"Reach in and get them," Coach Smith said.

Johnny asked, "Would you reach into a toilet for only two dollars?"

Coach Smith thought about it. "No," he finally said.

"Me neither," Johnny said. "That's why I'm mad."

Tom Morgan stood up. He was the other center on the Howling Timberwolves hockey team. It was his first season with the Timberwolves.

"I have an idea," Tom said. "I can help if Coach Smith says it is okay."

"Go ahead, Tom," Coach Smith said. "It would be better if Johnny were thinking about hockey instead of his money. This is an important game."

Tom looked at Johnny. "Could you give me your coat?"

"How will that help?" Johnny asked. But he handed his coat to Tom.

Tom walked across the dressing room in his skates. He pushed open the door to the toilet. Everyone on the team watched. Tom reached into the pocket of Johnny's coat and gathered up all the change he found. Then he dropped the change in the toilet.

"What did you do that for?" Johnny said. "That was all the rest of my money!"

"Yes," Tom said. "Now you *have* to put your hand in the toilet to get it. And while you are doing that, you can get the two loonies you lost too."

CHAPTER TWO

"Look!" Johnny said to his friend Stu Duncan. "See in the stands? That's Ian James!"

Stu and Johnny were in the players' bench. The referee was ready to drop the puck to start the third period of the game. The score was two to two against a team called the Calgary Rams. If the Timberwolves won the game, they would go on to the semi-finals.

"Ian James!" Stu said. "He's watching our game? Wow!"

Ian James was a defensemen for the Calgary Flames in the NHL.

"I wonder why he is here," Tom said.

"That must be his son on the other team," Stu said. "The name on the back of the sweater says James."

Then the whistle blew. Johnny and Stu went on the ice to start the game. They were going to play against the son of Ian James.

After the face-off, Johnny Maverick had the puck at center ice. He passed it to his left wing. Johnny skated fast to the blue line and yelled for a pass back. The left wing gave it to him.

Johnny faked that he was going to the left of the defenseman. Then he cut quickly to the right. He was around the defenseman! He had a breakaway!

Johnny fired a hard wrist shot. It went between the goalie's legs. A goal! The Timberwolves were ahead three to two.

"Great move!" Stu said as they skated back to the bench. "That was Ian James's son you beat."

The other line went on the ice for their shift. They made sure the Calgary Rams did not score.

Johnny Maverick went on the ice the next shift. The face-off was in the Timberwolves' end.

Johnny lost the face-off. The puck went back to the same defenseman he had beat the shift before. Johnny rushed toward the defenseman. Ian James's son took a shot that bounced off Johnny's shin pad toward center ice.

Johnny chased the puck. The defenseman fell down.

Johnny had another breakaway!

This time Johnny deked the goalie. He scored again! The Timberwolves were ahead four to two.

Then Johnny and Stu went back to the bench. The other line went on the ice for their shift. Once again they made sure the Calgary Rams did not score.

Johnny Maverick went on the ice again. This time the face-off was in the other team's end.

Johnny won the draw. He kicked the puck back to the Timberwolves defenseman. The defenseman took a shot at net.

Johnny was in front of the goal. He was trying to push the Calgary Rams defenseman out of the way. Johnny looked up in time to see the puck coming. He lifted his stick and deflected the puck into the net.

Another goal! The Timberwolves were ahead five to two.

The coach on the other team called for a time-out.

"That's three goals in three shifts," Stu said to Johnny when they got back to the bench. "A hat trick. And you scored them all against the son of Ian James!"

"Hey, Johnny," Tom said. He was standing near the boards. He heard what Stu said to Johnny. "Three goals. That should put you in a good mood. Maybe you won't be mad at me anymore for my little trick."

"You should listen to him," Stu told Johnny. "He did say sorry. Revenge is never a good idea. And remember, we are all friends, right?"

"I don't want revenge," Johnny said. "I just want to get even with him."

"Oh," Stu said. "Maybe next week in school you should learn what the word 'revenge' means."

Before Johnny could answer, the referee blew the whistle to start the game again. The other line was back on the ice. The Calgary Rams did not score against them.

In fact, that's the way the score stayed. When the buzzer rang at the end of the game, the Timberwolves had won five to two.

CHAPTER THREE

The team was in the dressing room, and everyone was excited about the win. Suddenly there was a knock on the door.

Coach Smith opened the door.

Everyone in the dressing room saw that it was Ian James, the professional hockey player. He was very big. He wore a Calgary Flames jacket.

"Hello," Coach Smith said.

"Hello, Coach," Ian James said. He stepped into the dressing room. He was carrying a hockey stick. He looked at all the players.

It was very quiet.

This was Ian James!

"Where is Johnny Maverick?" Ian said. "I want to talk to the hockey player who scored three goals against my son in three shifts."

Johnny Maverick stood up. The dressing room stayed very quiet.

"I hope you are not mad at me," Johnny said to Ian James.

"I am not mad at all," Ian James said. "I came here to tell you that I was very impressed with your hockey."

"Really?" Johnny said.

"Really," Ian James said. "In fact, I am impressed with the entire team. You all played good hockey. You beat my son's team fair and square. And you were good sports. I like to see that in minor hockey."

"Thank you," Coach Smith said.

"Thank you," everyone on the team said.

"I want to wish you all the best in the semi-finals," Ian James said. "And there is one other thing."

He held out the hockey stick.

"This stick has been signed by everyone on the

Calgary Flames hockey team," Ian James said. "I had it in my car."

"Wow!" Coach Smith said. "Look at this stick, you guys."

Coach Smith didn't have to say that. Everyone was looking. This was Ian James! The stick was signed by all the Calgary Flames players!

"I want to give this stick to Johnny Maverick," Ian James said. "He was the all-star of the game against my son's team."

"Really?" Johnny said.

"Really," Ian James said.

"Wow!" Johnny said.

"Wow!" everyone on the team said.

Then Ian James left.

"Good job," Coach Smith said to Johnny. "I'm glad for you."

Johnny was hugging the stick.

"I love this stick," he said. "I am going to call my parents and tell them as soon as we get to the hotel."

"You love the stick?" Tom Morgan said. "Are you going to sleep with it?"

Nearly everyone laughed. But Johnny didn't.

"You already played one trick on me," Johnny said. "But I'm too smart to let you do anything to this hockey stick."

"I was just making a joke about sleeping with it," Tom said. "And I said I was sorry about the other trick."

"I don't believe you," Johnny said. "So the answer is 'yes'."

"The answer to what?" Tom said.

"To your question," Johnny answered. "You asked if I was going to sleep with my hockey stick."

"Oh, that question," Tom said.

"I'm going to sleep with it," Johnny said. "I'm going to eat with it. I'm going to shower with it."

"Sleep and eat and shower with it?" Tom said.

"That's right," Johnny said. "You might play another trick on me, but there is no way in the world you are going to get this hockey stick away from me. And that's a promise."

CHAPTER FOUR

The Howling Timberwolves went to a restaurant after the game. Johnny and Stu sat at a table with Tom and Coach Smith. Johnny had his hockey stick with him. The rest of the team sat at tables nearby.

When the waitress stopped to take their orders, she said, "That's a hockey stick. You're not planning to play hockey in here, are you?" She was making a joke.

"I'm guarding it," Johnny said. "I'm going to sleep and eat and shower with it. I love this stick. Nobody is going to do anything to my stick!"

The waitress laughed. She thought Johnny was making a joke too.

When the food arrived Coach Smith was away from the table. He was calling the parents in Howling to let them know the team was in the semi-finals.

Johnny had ordered pancakes and sausages. He put some syrup on a side plate. Then he put a piece of butter in the middle of the syrup.

"What are you doing?" Stu asked Johnny.

"I heard that butter gets hot if you put salt on it," Johnny answered. "I want to see if it's true."

"That's crazy," Tom said. "Putting salt on butter doesn't make it hot."

"You're probably right," Johnny said. "But I want to find out for myself."

Johnny poured a little bit of salt on the butter.

He opened his hand and put his palm right over top of the butter. He waited. He looked at Stu.

"Tom is right, Stu," Johnny said. "It doesn't get hot. I don't feel a thing."

"Maybe try some more salt," Stu said.

18

Johnny put more salt on the butter. He opened his hand again and put his palm over the butter.

"Nothing," he told Stu. "I don't feel any heat."

"Of course not," Tom said. "I told you it was crazy. You're dumb to think it would work."

"Well," Johnny said, "maybe it doesn't make the butter hot enough to boil water. Maybe you need to get your hand as close as possible to feel it."

Johnny lowered his open palm until it was almost on the plate.

"Hey!" Johnny said. "I'm right. Tom is wrong. I can feel the heat."

"No way," Tom said. "That's crazy."

"You try it," Johnny told Tom. "Then we'll see who is right."

"I'm right," Tom said. He reached across the table. "Move your hand, Johnny."

Johnny pulled his hand away.

Tom opened his hand. He put his palm directly above the butter. "I don't feel anything."

"It doesn't make the butter hot enough to boil water," Johnny told Tom. "You have to have your hand really close."

"This close?" Tom lowered his hand so it was almost touching the butter.

"Close enough," Johnny said. Then he quickly pushed Tom's hand down into the plate. He squished Tom's hand into the butter and the syrup.

"Hey!" Tom said.

Tom lifted his hand. It was sticky from the butter and the syrup.

Everyone on the team began to laugh at Tom.

"Now we're even," Johnny said. "You made me put my hand in the toilet. And I made you put your hand in the syrup."

"Even!" Tom was mad because everyone was laughing. "I don't think so. Just wait until I get you back!"

"Guys," Stu told them. "Revenge is never a good idea. And we are all friends. Remember?"

"Revenge?" Tom said. "I don't want revenge."

"Let me guess," Stu said. "You just want to get even."

"Exactly," Tom said. "So Johnny better watch out. Because something really might happen to his Ian James hockey stick."

CHAPTER FIVE

The score was four to three. The Timberwolves were losing to the Calgary Hawks in the semi-final game. If the Timberwolves lost, they were out of the tournament. If they won, they would stay the night in Calgary. The finals would be the next morning.

But there was only five minutes left in the game. The Timberwolves needed two goals to win.

"This doesn't look good," Johnny said to Stu. They were on the bench, waiting for their shift.

"No," Stu said. "Maybe I shouldn't have eaten all those pancakes at the restaurant."

"You mean today?" Johnny asked his friend. "Or all your life?"

"Hah, hah," Stu said. "Aren't you funny."

"Yes, I—" Johnny stopped. He was watching the game. "Oh no. Our goalie just tripped their center. Our team is going to get a penalty."

Now the Timberwolves were a man short. This was big trouble. Coach Smith sent Johnny and Stu out, along with Tom.

The Calgary Hawks moved the puck into the Timberwolves end. Stu went into the corner to get the puck. He fell. As he was sliding along the ice, he swung for the puck with his stick. It bounced off the boards, right onto Tom's stick. Tom saw a defenseman in front of him. He shot the puck off the boards around the defenseman to center ice. Tom raced as hard as he could to get the loose puck.

He got past the defenseman. Suddenly, he had a breakaway!

Halfway to the goal, the other defenseman tried to trip Tom. But Tom managed to stay on his skates. He skated hard toward the goalie. He fired a high wrist shot into the top of the net.

The Timberwolves had scored!

Now it was four all. But there were only three minutes left.

Johnny and Stu and Tom skated by the bench.

"Can you stay on the ice?" Coach Smith asked them.

Tom nodded. He went back to the center ice to take the face-off. Johnny and Stu stayed on the ice too.

The referee dropped the puck. The Hawks center won the draw. The puck went to the left defense. Tom didn't chase the puck. He waited near the center.

Johnny charged forward at the defenseman with the puck. Tom watched carefully. He saw that the left defense was going to pass to the right defense. He waited to the last second. Then he charged ahead just as the left defense began to pass across the ice.

Tom intercepted the pass!

He had another breakaway.

This time the defenseman tripped him. Tom slid on his stomach, watching the puck go into the corner.

When the Hawks defenseman touched the puck, the whistle blew.

The referee called a penalty.

Tom got up on his skates again. He saw that everyone was looking at him.

Johnny skated close to Tom.

"Good job," Johnny said. "The referee is going to give you a penalty shot."

"What?"

"A penalty shot. If you score, we will be ahead."

Tom took a deep breath. He looked like he was nervous.

The referee placed the puck at center ice. It was quiet in the arena. The referee blew the whistle.

Tom took the puck and slowly skated up the ice. He crossed the blue line and picked up speed.

The goalie came out of the net to make sure Tom didn't have much to shoot at.

Tom faked left. He went right. Then left again. The goalie fell for the move. Tom rolled the puck to his backhand and lifted it into the open net.

Five to four!

Tom lifted his hands high in the air. The crowd cheered.

Three minutes later, the game was over. The Timberwolves had won.

Tom and Johnny skated off the ice together.

"I scored three goals in three shifts to win the last game," Johnny said to Tom. "Now you helped us win this game. Do you think that makes us even?"

"Not a chance," Tom said. "Now we're staying another night. So I have a lot of time to get you, don't I? Just watch out, because something might happen to your Ian James hockey stick."

CHAPTER SIX

"I don't think this is a good idea," Stu said to Johnny.

They were walking down the hallway of the hotel. No one else was there. Johnny had a can of shaving cream in one hand. He had a big envelope in the other. Stu carried Johnny's hockey stick. Johnny was not going to let that stick get out of his sight.

"You said that five times already," Johnny whispered back. "But I notice you are still here with me. I think you really want to see me play this trick on Tom."

"No," Stu said. "I'm here to try to stop you. Revenge is never a good idea. We are all friends, remember?"

"I have to get even with Tom."

"You're already even," Stu said. "This would put you ahead in tricks."

"He said he was going to do something to my hockey stick," Johnny said. "I need to get ahead before he tries something."

"Revenge is never a good idea," Stu said. "The war will never end. And what if he does something to your hockey stick?"

"No," Johnny said. "I'm going to—"

"I know," Stu said. "You're going to sleep and eat and shower with it."

"Yes."

They stopped in front of the door to room 207.

"Watch this," Johnny said.

Johnny opened the envelope and filled it with shaving cream. Then he put it on the floor. He pushed the open end of the envelope a little ways under the door.

"This is great," Johnny whispered. "When Tom comes to answer the door, I'll stomp on the envelope and shoot shaving cream all over him."

"Please don't do this," Stu said. "Revenge is not a good idea. Besides, I don't think it will work. The shaving cream won't shoot high enough. It will only hit his feet."

It was too late. Johnny had already knocked on the door.

Johnny raised his voice to sound like a woman. "Room service," he said in a high voice.

He knocked again.

Stu and Johnny heard footsteps on the other side of the door. Then they heard the sound of the bolt moving.

"Now!" Johnny whispered.

He stomped as hard as he could on the envelope. *Whoosh.* Then he quickly leaned down and pulled the envelope away and tucked it into his pants behind his back.

"Hah!" Johnny said.

Then the door opened.

But it was not Tom. It was a woman with bright red hair. She was wearing a housecoat and she had shaving cream all over the front of her slippers. She also did not look at all pleased.

"See?" Stu said. "I told you revenge isn't a good idea."

Chapter Seven

The woman in the housecoat stepped into the hallway.

"What is going on here?" she asked. "That is exactly what I would like to know. I see a boy with a can of shaving cream in his hand. I don't even want to know why the other boy is holding a hockey stick."

Just then Johnny and Stu saw Tom walking down the hall toward them.

"Hey guys," he said. "What's happening?"

"I think I should go," Stu said. He tried to hand the hockey stick back to Johnny. "It was nice knowing you, Johnny."

Johnny didn't take the stick. He grabbed Stu's sleeve so he couldn't run away.

Tom said, "Hey, Johnny, why did you spray shaving cream on this nice woman's slippers?"

The woman looked down. She saw the shaving cream on her slippers.

"What?!? My slippers!"

Johnny looked at the woman. He pointed at Tom. "I was trying to play a trick on him."

"Do I look like him?" the woman asked.

She was big, and she had shaving cream on her slippers. She also looked as mean as a buffalo. She definitely didn't look like Tom.

Johnny told the truth. "No, you don't look like Tom. But I thought he was in room 207. That's the room they gave him at the front desk. I was listening when they gave him the key."

"But you can see you were wrong," the woman said.

"I can see that now," Johnny said. He was glad that Stu had his hockey stick. He was glad that the woman did *not* have it. "I am very sorry for stomping shaving cream under your door."

The woman frowned. "I should tell your parents about this."

"My parents aren't here," Johnny said. "We are here with a hockey team."

Tom said to the woman, "I can tell you what room our coach is in if you want to talk to him instead. Then our coach will talk to his parents."

"Thanks," Johnny said to Tom. But he didn't mean it.

"You boys are lucky my favorite TV show is about to come on," the woman said. "Otherwise I *would* talk to your coach."

She slammed the door shut.

"That was very funny," Tom said. "It's too bad for you we had to switch rooms."

"Switch rooms?" Johnny said. Johnny hit his forehead with his hand. "You switched rooms?"

"Sure," Tom said. "This one is a smoking room. They gave it to us by mistake. So we had to go back and get another room."

"See?" Stu said to Johnny. "I told you the shaving cream wasn't a good idea. Besides, it didn't work. All you did was get her slippers."

"It was a great idea," Tom said. "Just wait until I tell the whole team what happened. That lady looked really mad. This will get a big laugh."

"You're right," Johnny said to Stu. "Maybe the shaving cream wasn't such a good idea."

"Neither is revenge," Stu said. "Remember. We are all friends."

CHAPTER EIGHT

Johnny and Stu got back to the hotel room. It was time to go to sleep.

"Are you really going to sleep with that hockey stick?" Stu asked Johnny.

"Yes. I'm going to eat with it and sleep with it and shower with it. It is not getting out of my sight."

"If you shower with it," Stu said, "you might wash off the players' signatures."

"Good thinking," Johnny said. "Okay, I won't shower with it. But I'm going to eat with it and sleep with it."

Stu shut off the lights and got into his bed.

Johnny got into his bed on the other side of the room. He put his stick under the covers with him.

"Hey!" Johnny said in the darkness. "What is this?"

Stu got out of bed. He turned on the lights.

Johnny was sitting up in bed. His feet and hands and the side of his face were sticky.

"Honey!" Johnny said. "It's on my pillow! It's on my sheets! I'm a mess!"

"How did honey get there?" Stu asked.

Johnny noticed a piece of paper sticking out from under his pillow. It was a note. He pulled it out. He read it to Stu.

"'I wanted you and your hockey stick to have sweet dreams'," Johnny said.

"Is the note signed?" Stu asked.

"Yes," Johnny said.

"It's not from Coach Smith, is it?" Stu said.

"No," Johnny said. "It's from Tom. He put the honey in my bed."

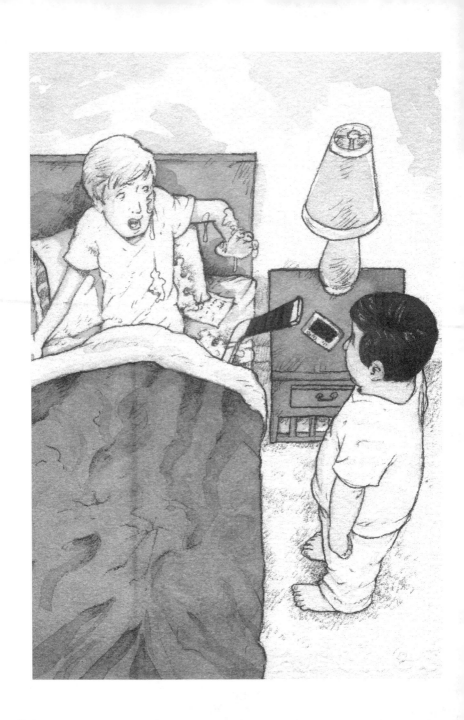

"Johnny," Stu said. "Now you are really behind. You sprayed shaving cream on a woman's slippers. He got honey in your bed while you were trying to get him. It would be a good idea to call a truce."

"No," Johnny said. "I've got an idea. There is a store beside the hotel. Tomorrow I'll buy honey to put in his skates and in his hockey gloves."

"Please don't," Stu said. "Think of our team."

"Our team?"

"It would be nice to win the tournament. You shouldn't do anything that will cause the team to lose. Remember. We are all friends."

"I know, I know," Johnny said. "And revenge is never a good idea. But I don't want revenge. I just want to get even."

Stu sighed. "Someday maybe you will understand that getting even is revenge. Maybe you will also learn it is never a good idea."

"You're right," Johnny said.

"I'm glad you agree."

"You're right that it would be nice to win the tournament," Johnny said. "I'll have to find a way to get even with Tom after the game."

Stu sighed again. "And what about the stick?"

"My stick?"

"So far he has only played tricks on you. What if he finds a way to do something to your Ian James hockey stick?"

"Never," Johnny said. "I'm going to eat with it and sleep with it. But not shower with it. I promise you. There is no way in the world he will even do anything to my Ian James hockey stick."

"Just remember one thing," Stu said.

"That we are all friends? That revenge is never a good idea?"

"That when something happens to your stick," Stu answered, "I am going to be the first one to say I told you so."

CHAPTER NINE

The score was four to three. The Timberwolves were leading the Calgary Cougars. They were just about to start the final period of the final hockey game of the tournament. If the Howling Timberwolves won, they would be the tournament champions.

"Hey, how did you get into my room last night?" Johnny asked Tom as they skated back out onto the ice.

"Easy," Tom said. "I just asked for another key. The guy behind the desk saw my hockey jacket. He probably thought I was you."

"Oh," Johnny said.

"Are you still going to try to get even?" Tom asked.

"It's more important that we win this game," Johnny said. "Besides, remember what Stu said: We are all friends."

"Then let's win the game," Tom said.

The Timberwolves played good defense and managed to keep the Cougars from scoring another goal.

Now there was only three minutes left in the game.

After a face-off, the puck went into end of the Timberwolves. Johnny waited for a pass. When the puck came to him, he tried to stickhandle by the Cougar center. The Cougar center was not fast enough to stop Johnny. So he reached ahead and tripped Johnny with his stick.

Penalty!

Coach Smith waved for Johnny and Stu to get off the ice because they were tired.

Tom won the face-off in the Cougars' end. The puck went back to the defenseman. A Cougar forward charged toward the defenseman. The defenseman couldn't get a shot on the net. He fired the puck toward the corner. The puck skipped past a couple of players and went to Tom, who was standing behind the net.

Tom pretended he was going to go one way. The goalie went to that side of the net. Tom quickly went

the other way. Before the goalie could get to the other side of the net, Tom had reached around and scored. It was a wrap-around goal!

The Timberwolves were ahead five to three!

Time ran out for the Calgary Cougars. The Timberwolves had won the tournament!

In the dressing room after the game, the players were very excited. There was a lot of noise and backslapping. Everyone was talking about the big plays that had won the game.

Johnny dressed quickly. He didn't seem to be as excited as his teammates. He looked around the room and saw that no one was watching him. He stepped outside and ran down the hallway. He opened the door that led outside.

He reached into the snow and pulled out a plastic bag that he had hidden there before the game.

Hah, Johnny thought. *This will get Tom back.*

Chapter Ten

The bus ride from Calgary to Howling took about two hours. By the time they were getting close to home, the boys were tired of celebrating their win. The bus had been quiet for about ten minutes.

"Hey, does anybody smell anything weird?" Tom said. He'd been sleeping for the past half hour.

"Yes, I do smell something," Johnny said.

The other players all looked away so that Tom could not see them smile. Johnny had told all of them about his latest trick.

"What do you smell?" Tom asked.

"I smell a winning team!" said Johnny Maverick.

All the other players laughed.

"No," Tom said. He sniffed the air. "It stinks! It smells like fish."

"You must be imagining things," Johnny said. "Why would there be fish in a hockey bus?"

Tom sniffed the air again. "This is very strange."

He closed his eyes again and tried to go back to sleep.

"See?" Johnny whispered to Stu. "Nothing went wrong. And I still have my Ian James hockey stick."

"Just wait," Stu said. "Revenge is never a good idea."

Tom sat up again. He sniffed the air.

"Guys," he said. "I'm telling you. I smell fish."

This was too much for the other players. They all began to laugh.

"What?" Tom said. "What?"

"Remember the loonies and toonies you took from my coat pocket and dropped in the toilet?" Johnny asked him.

"Yes."

"Well, I put something back in your pocket."

Tom reached into his coat pocket. He pulled his hands out very quickly.

Everyone laughed again.

Tom smelled his fingers. "Fish? In my pocket?"

"Sardines!" Johnny said. "I bought them before the game. They were frozen at the start of the trip. But they thawed out just like I planned." All the other players laughed. Even Coach Smith. Coach Smith was in a good mood because the team had won.

"Very, very funny," Tom said. "But you'd better watch out. There is still time for me to do something to your Ian James hockey stick."

"Not a chance," Johnny said. "I'm not going to let it out of my sight. Besides, look ahead. There are the lights of Howling now. We're almost home. What could you possibly do now?"

CHAPTER ELEVEN

When the bus stopped at the rink, Johnny looked out the window. He could see all of the parents were waiting under the lights. Coach Smith had phoned ahead to let everyone know that the Howling Timberwolves had won the tournament. Even Mayor Thorpe was there.

The players stepped off the bus. Johnny, of course, was still holding his Ian James hockey stick.

"Hah," Johnny said to Tom. "I told you. It's too late to get even now."

Before Tom could say anything back to Johnny, Coach Smith spoke to the whole team.

"Line up, guys," Coach Smith said. "Mayor Thorpe wants to give each of you a town pin for winning the trophy."

Johnny lined up with the rest of the players. Tom stood beside Johnny. Johnny was the only player holding a hockey stick. He was not going to let go of it. He was still afraid that Tom might try something.

One by one, Mayor Thorpe shook hands with each player and gave each a pin.

When Mayor Thorpe reached Johnny, he gave him a pin and shook his hand.

"Good job," Mayor Thorpe said. "I heard that you scored three goals in three shifts against the son of Ian James."

"Yes," Johnny said. " He even came into our dressing room after the game."

"I heard that too," Mayor Thorpe said. "And I heard he gave you a stick that is signed by all the Calgary Flames."

"Yes," Johnny said. "This is it."

"May I look at the stick?" Mayor Thorpe asked.

Johnny gave him the stick.

"This is wonderful," Mayor Thorpe said. "Imagine, a stick signed by all the Calgary Flames. If I had something like that, I would hang it in my office."

"Mayor Thorpe?" Tom spoke up from beside Johnny. "I think you will be very happy."

"Why?" Mayor Thorpe asked.

"Well," Tom said, "on the bus Johnny and I were talking about you and what a good job you do as mayor in our town."

"Thank you," Mayor Thorpe said.

"You're welcome," Tom said. "You will be very happy to know that Johnny told me he wanted to give you that stick for you to hang in your office."

Before Johnny could say anything, the Mayor shouted to all the parents.

"Look at this!" Mayor Thorpe said. He held up the Ian James hockey stick for everyone to look at. "Johnny Maverick gave me the Ian James hockey stick to hang up in my office!"

All the parents clapped. All of the hockey players started laughing.

Mayor Thorpe shook Johnny's hand. "Thank you! Thank you!" Mayor Thorpe said. "This is the best thing I can imagine!"

Mayor Thorpe walked away. He brought the stick over to the other parents so they could look at it.

"I can't believe it," Johnny Maverick said to Tom. "I can't believe it. My stick. It's gone."

All of the other players were still laughing.

Stu looked at Johnny.

"I have four words for you," Stu said.

"What?" Johnny said.

"I told you so."

"You're right," Johnny told Stu.

"Don't worry," Tom said. "Tomorrow I'll go to Mayor Thorpe's office and tell him I played a trick on you. I'm sure he will understand. You'll get your stick back then."

"No," Johnny said. "He should keep it. That way I'll never forget that Stu was right. Revenge is never a good idea!"

"Getting even isn't a good idea either," Tom said.

Johnny stuck out his hand.

"Truce?" Johnny asked.

"Truce," Tom said. They shook hands. "So I better tell you something."

"Yes?" Johnny said.

"Remember the sardines you put in my coat pocket?" Tom asked.

"Yes," Johnny said. "How could I forget?"

"I put them in your duffel bag when you weren't looking," Tom said. "You'd better take them out before you get home."

Sigmund Brouwer is the best-selling author of many books for children and young adults. He has contributed to the Orca Currents series (*Wired, Sewer Rats*) and the Orca Sports series, which also debuts this fall.

Sigmund enjoys visiting schools to talk about his books. Interested teachers can find out more by e-mailing authorbookings@coolreading.com.

Also Available:
TIMBERWOLF CHASE

Johnny Maverick and his friends play for the Timberwolves peewee hockey team in the small town of Howling. Tom Morgan has just moved from Toronto and is a talented player. Tom is also very competitive and seems determined to pick on Stu Duncan, who is slightly overweight. Johnny suggests a race between Tom and Stu. Tom eagerly accepts; Stu is reluctant, but Johnny convinces him to trust his best friend's advice. On race day Tom is surprised by both the race and its outcome and learns that teamwork pays off.